Reflections Of A Hunter's Wife

June Belcher-Veasley

Entegrity Choice Publishing
PO Box 453
Powder Springs, GA 30127
info@entegritypublishing.com
www.entegritypublishing.com
770.727.6517

Printed in the United States of America

The views expressed in this work are solely those of the author
and do not necessarily reflect the views of the publisher, and
the publisher hereby disclaims any responsibility for them. The
publisher is not responsible for websites (or their content) that
are not owned by the publisher.

Library of Congress Cataloging-in-Publication Data
ISBN 978-1-7330301-4-4
Library of Congress Control Number: 2019915897

Dedication

I dedicate these tales to my husband for his many humorous adventures while hunting.

Contents

Dedication 3

Introduction
The Beginning Behind the
Reflections. 7

Reflections 1
He Begins 9

Reflections 2
OOOH What a Night! 13

Reflections 3
He Falls Down 21

Reflections 4
The Eating of Common
Snapper 27

Reflection 5
    He Was Lost, But Now
    He's Found 33

Reflections 6
    He's Hanging Out! 39

Reflections 7
    He'll Shop Til' He Drops 47

Reflections 8
    It's Guarding the Homestead 57

Reflections 9
    He's Exploring New Territory 61

Reflections 10
    He Concludes 67

The Beginning Behind the Reflections

Our history began when we were children. We met on the Southside of Atlanta, Georgia, in the projects called Carver Homes. We were about thirteen or fourteen years of age.

It was during the seventies. Significant events were taking place in the city; it was a changing time for the people in my community and all the people of color in the south. Our families did pass on their struggles as well as their positivity. Both families moved out of the projects and relocated on the east side of the city of Atlanta, in now Dekalb County. During this time many black families were transiting out of the city limits and into the suburbs.

Years passed, and by chance, we ran into each other on a warm summer day in downtown Atlanta. During that chance meeting, we decided to date. We talked for a little while longer; later we parted company. As I arrived home, I realized that he did not get any information from me as to where I lived, nor did he ask for a phone number. He just walked away and went on his way. As time passed by, my mind went on to planning for the next possible date. Planning for the next chance encounter never happened because he found me. I was pleasantly surprised.

As I sit and reflect on our lives together, we have journeyed for over thirty-five years. Several of the years were downs, but we have had more ups than downs. So, I sit here, reflecting upon some of the many ups of our long life together. My first journey begins with my husband's hunting escapades. So, sit down, read, and laugh at some of my hunter's wife reflections.

Reflections 1
He Begins

Well, it's fall again. Hunters get to practice and implement their hunting prowess for bagging a buck (deer). Once again, the air is crisp, and the birds are chirping. The leaves are just turning colors. You can see the reds, browns, orange, and yellow leaves blowing in the breeze. You can feel the seasonal change in the air. It feels marvelous breathing in the fresh fall air.

Standing in my kitchen and looking out of the window, I began to reflect upon the practices that my husband implements when the fall season starts. He opens his ritual in the following manner:

"Hey babe, where is my green hunting trunk with the Marine emblem on it?

"It's in the hall closet."

"I don't see it." He zipped from one closet to another throughout the house. These searches consist of running throughout the house and pulling out trunks of hunting paraphernalia. I can always tell when he looks through his vehicle by the loud clanking sounds of things he tosses aside and out on to the ground. "I need that," bang!! There it goes, rolling as if it was thrown from the other side of his favorite hunting pickup.

"I don't need that." He places it in the back of his personal vehicle, into its unique location in the blue bomber truck. "I might need that." He places each item in a neat pile in the front yard. "I will save this for another trip." This process went on for at least three days. After more than twenty years of marriage, I have gotten used to seeing this hunter's dance.

As he danced the dance of the hunting preparation, the front and backyard became a vision of piles of hunting gear in small mounts with different things in each one. These many items usually range from deer piss to several hunting rifles.

Reflections 2
OOOH
What a Night!

As this ritual would proceed, I would watch and wait for him to prepare for the three-day hunting trip. As I watch and wait, I reflected upon several of his incidents: one such event was when he had a dream that I was a buck to be bagged (killed and eaten). Mind you; he often spoke in his sleep, especially after a hunting trip. On this particular evening, he was in rare form.

One evening, on a crisp November night,

Carl and I prepared to settle down for a good night's sleep.

"Goodnight, "said Carl.

I respond in kind, "Goodnight."

As we both said our goodnights, we snuggled down underneath a thick, cozy comforter. Before long, we were sound asleep.

We couldn't have been asleep very long before I was awakened with,

"Kill it, Killlllll it!

Johnny kill it! Johnnnnnnnyyyyyy kill it?" He yells.

I awake immediately. I sit up, look around. To my surprise, I hear and see that my husband is shouting in his sleep. His tossing and turning and yelling were astonishing. To me, it seems as if he was acting out an event that took place on one of their hunting trips.

"My, what could have triggered this behavior?" I thought.

Johnny is the name he is yelling. He is my husband's first cousin. They hunt together quite often. They have killed deer, turtles, pheasants, quail, and rabbit for over 30 years. If it was edible, they killed it, cooked it and ate it; all but possum. Somehow Carl couldn't stomach that critter.

Johnny prepares for hunting too. He would go through the same essential preparation. How I know this is because they would call each other and talk for hours. They would check and recheck their itinerary down to the last piece of the necessary equipment that they needed. I've yet to witness Johnny display any of them to me. I usually learn about them from Carl.

After a few startling moments pass, I realize that we didn't leave the television on nor a radio again, since having the TV on was a common occurrence. To my dismay, this disturbance was not coming from the video; instead, it was coming from my husband Carl. I pinpointed the noise; I turned around to see my husband thrashing about on the bed. I eased from the bed.

He suddenly jumps up.

Swoosh!

Off go the covers on the floor. Carl moved his arms as if he was loading a rife.

"Carl!" I called to my husband. "Carl!"

"Carl, wake up!" I yelled again.

He appeared to be in a hypnotic sleep. I watched him as I eased over closer to the bedroom door. Minutes ticked by as I watched him warily.

Looking on in shock, he began aiming his invisible weapon in my direction. I was shocked to realize that he thought that I was a deer. I was possibly a ten-point buck that he and his cousin Johnny have been trying to bag for sometimes now.

"Carl, please wake up!" I called again.

He followed me with his eyes and his

deer hunter's stance. I paused, like a deer caught in headlights. I felt paralyzed during my husband's night dream. I did not find humor in this situation; I feared that he would shoot, gut, and chop me into pieces, and even store me in the deep freezer later for eating or distributing to every relative in the metropolitan area.

Moving ever so slowly, but nearer to the bedroom door, I yell out, "Wake up, Carl! Wake up!"

Once again, I pleaded for him to wake up. In desperation, I yell even louder. Sometimes he was a little hard of hearing.

"Please, wake up! You're asleep! You are at home and not on a hunting trip; wake up!"

After finally making my plea heard, he suddenly stops, puts his imaginary gun down, and climbs back into bed. Before long, I could listen to and see that he was back asleep. Realizing that he was once again asleep, I wholly composed myself. I could not believe he returned to bed and was sound asleep as if nothing had happened.

The next morning was an uneventful one. I arose and started my usual routine. I expected Carl to be up and talking about what had happened the night before, but he was still asleep. As I stepped out of the bedroom, I looked again at my sleeping husband. I smiled and shook my head as I closed the bedroom door. I moved slowly but quietly to the kitchen to prepare breakfast.

During breakfast, I broached the subject of his (hunting dream) from the previous night. "Babe, are you all right?" I asked.

"What?" He replied.

"The dream," I said softly.

I tried to convince him of what had happened the night before. He just chuckled and removed himself from the kitchen. I shook my head as he walked out of the kitchen.

The kids continued to eat their breakfast, paying the adults little attention. He goes on to say, "I don't remember a dream. I slept like a baby."

He looks at me and says, "If I had done that, I would remember."

He continued to state that he had no recollection of anything that happened last night. He paused from consuming his meal. He looks up suddenly and we gazed at each other for several seconds. Carl says, "If that really happened, I would remember it." I continued gazing at him as he resumed eating his meal.

I glance around noting that our kids were still consuming their breakfast.

Saying to myself, "Oh! What a night to remember."

Reflections 3
He Falls Down

If memory serves me right, this incident could not begin to compare with Carl's other hunting adventures. One day while hunting with his cousin Johnny, he fell out of a tall pine tree, head first. He misjudged the strength or durability of the tree. Dropping out of a tall tree headfirst could have been his last hunting trip.

The story goes like this. While hunting in late November on a cold, but early sunny morning, they both set forth to earn a hunting notch on their belt. I have learned that these notches are bragging rights among hunters. While sharing his tale, I was surprised to hear that my husband fell out of a tree; it was unbelievable since he was a very experienced hunter and has hunted for most of his life. I couldn't comprehend that this had happened to him. I've known my husband for over 25 years; this just doesn't happen to him.

"Carl, falling out of a tree - NO WAY!" I thought.

As he related the tale to me, I listened with disbelief to his recanting of such a story of the great fall.

He begins: "Johnny and I prepared our hunting trip on a cold frigid fall day. It was cold as hell. You know, I like cold weather," he states with a broad smile on his face.

"Cold weather is the best time to hunt deer. It was thirty degrees outside. Whew! Man!" He goes on to say, "Johnny and I went hunting in central Georgia."

"Where did you all hunt in central Georgia?" I asked.

"West Point," he replied. "We were working on bagging a deer.

Hopefully, we were planning to bring home a buck. Johnny brought along his doe urine. That's a guaranteed buck lure. They will come from near and far to mate with a doe once they get a sniff of this stuff. Pow!!!! Fresh cut deer steaks soon and good eating too."

"We use it all the time to attract the large male bucks. Boy, you don't want to get between a rutting buck and a doe; they would kill you. We also do a few other preparatory things too. We carry with us two skinning knives and some extra hunting camouflage fatigues," he states. He went on with beguiling me with his tale for some time.

Time passed as we continued sitting in the kitchen drinking cups of coffee as his story hummed steadily along.

"You know babe; once we were in the woods, we would separate. One time we separated to scout more ground. I ran upon some deer tacks. I followed them for a little distance, but I lost the animal tracks. I circled the area, but I did not recapture the scent. I scanned the surrounding for any animal droppings. I went quickly over the field without missing a step. I walked briskly in hopes that I would spot a prime target, a deer.

I walked for some distance and time, but no luck. So, after a while, I decided to climb a tree in hopes of spotting a deer. Up I went. Slowly, I progressed nearly to the top of a tall pine. I found a firm branch to balance and sit on. It was perfect for scouting deer. I called it my deer perch." He laughs. "Sitting nestled in the tree, I became content. I begin to nod off. Crash! I was so startled by the sudden noise that I forgot where I was for a moment. I jumped up from my position, failing to brace myself in the tree. Immediately, I lost my balance and pivoted head first out of the tree. I fell with my arms flailing through the air, legs kicking out, and my head aimed like a spear thrown to the ground. Thug! Plop! Wham! I fell into a pile of leaves."

Carl stops talking and looks over at my facial expression and laughs out loud.

My face reflected pure shock and horror. "What was he doing and thinking?" I thought to myself.

He looks at me and says, "I realize the severity of what happened, but I did survive it. Babe, I thank the Lord every day for the stupid things that I've done and the stupid things that I will do. I know that I could have broken my neck."

He laughs again at the idea of falling out of a tree, as he continues to regale me with his accounting of what happened to him. I have always known that I married a hunter.

My husband will still hunt, no matter what horrifying tales he shares during family gatherings.

As I think back, I reflect upon the many hunting tales that he has shared with me and the family. Carl will and has been a serious hunter. He seems to value his time with nature through practice, patience, and pride. But falling out of a tall pine tree did not stop him. He'll get up, dust himself off and plan for the next go-round of the hunting season with his cousin Johnny. My husband Carl has endured many mishaps while hunting with his cousin. Talking in his sleep and falling out of a tall pine tree are just a few episodes.

The Eating of Common Snapper

Carl's episodes were many, including the time he got lost on his family acreage in Camp Hill, Alabama. My husband prides himself on knowing the land which his family inherited years ago. He would tell me that as a young boy, he and his cousins would go into the woods and spend hours just scouting the land for various kinds of animals. They scouted and hunted rabbit, quail, pheasants, fish, and even turtle. One day he brought home from a scouting trip an enormous snapping turtle.

He says to me, "Hey baby, look at what I got. It nearly bit my toe-off."

I responded with, "Is that a turtle? "

"Yeah, it sure is," Carl says."

"Poor, poor, poor boy!"

"Carl, let him go, babe. Look, it's crying. Let it go!"

Mind you; I am used to having turtles as pets, not as a meal.

"Not this big boy!" Carl said.

"Carl, please, let it go." I asked again.

"No babe, this is going to be some good eating tonight," he states.

I was so flustered that I demanded he take it outside. He did, but not before he made the move to explain what had happened.

He states, "Babe, I moved my foot just in the nick of time. I nearly stepped on this big sucker. It's a big motherfu##," he started to say.

"Don't you dare say it, Carl. You better watch your language. Look, it is still alive," I said. "Barely."

He retorted with, "I am going to cut it up and have roasted turtle meat. I can make a stew. Wouldn't you like some?"

"Poor turtle," I said.

He breaks out into a full-throated laugh as he walks out of the house with the huge snapping turtle.

I yell after him, "Don't gut that helpless animal in the front yard."

I got no reply as seconds passed. Hours later, Carl returns to the house with a bowl of turtle meat. Glancing at it, it didn't look bad. It was pink and small.

I said, "That's not much meat."

My husband replied, "It's enough, for me. Would you like some of this meat?"

I said, "Yes, I would like to taste some."

He said, "You are going to love it."

I said, "We will see."

He commences cooking his turtle meat. He soaked it in fresh herbs to help draw out the wild taste. Next, he added the following ingredients to the animal flesh: garlic, meat tenderizer, salt, pepper, onions, bell pepper, flour, and a dash of cayenne pepper. My husband is also a great cook. He can grill a mean deer steak or a rabbit leg with baked potatoes.

The aroma of the cooking meat permeated the whole house. My mouth watered as I continued to smell the tantalizing scent of the roasting meat. By the time the animal parts were ready to eat, our kids had been fed and put to bed for the evening. It was just Carl and me sitting in the dining room eating the grilled turtle.

"MMMM, this is good," I said.

My husband just looked at me and smiled.

He said, "I told you that it would be good. I am a master chef," he teased.

We both chuckled and continued to consume the flavorful meat and potatoes as we talked about our day.

Reflection 5

He Was Lost, But Now He's Found

The next day was uneventful because we were coming to the end of the hunting season. I had to admit that the turtle meat that we had the night before was delicious. I did say a prayer for the poor turtle.

I said, "Thank you, Lord, for the gift of the master turtle for giving up his life so that I could eat."

As time passed on, Carl began the process of storing away his hunting gear and practices for his next hunting expedition. As he walked around the house, he began to relay a story about a time in which he had gotten lost. Lost, mind you, my husband, who considers himself a human GPS; I found it hard to believe. He never gets lost. My Carl would not allow himself to get lost, not while hunting on his family land. He would not permit himself to become missing on a piece of land that he visits each year with his family and friends. I asked him to tell me about this lost adventure.

He started like this; "It was a cold fall morning on Cousin Christine's farm. Christine's farm consists of chickens, pigs, lots of dogs, and a few cows. She did not have indoor plumbing, but she did have plenty of cold well water. On this particular day, I took off southbound into the thick woods that set behind her house. I walked for about three hours before I realized I had not packed my compass. I looked around to get my bearings, but I couldn't figure out which direction I should go. So, I stayed on the same path for at least a couple more hours. I walked until the sundown. It started to get dark. I still couldn't figure out how to get back on the right path. I walked for more than eight hours. I was tired.

By the time I reached a small hill on the property, it had become dark. I proceeded carefully so as not to fall, get hurt, or even lost (so you would think) while moving along the grounds. I could only see my hands in front of my face because of the intense darkness. I felt around in my backpack for an emergency light. Yes, it was right where I placed it, but somehow, I did not pack my navigator. What was I thinking?"

He said to himself, "I am Carl, human GPS."

He laughs at himself, and I chuckle along with him. He continued his tale of being lost in the woods.

Carl says, "I pulled out my flashlight and looked around. I learned that, if you are ever in the woods and you get lost, you should follow the Indian or the old way of tracking your directions. So, I looked and found moss on the trees, and it showed the direction that I needed to go. I looked around, found the right path, and made it safely out of the woods. I sure thought that I was going to be spending the night in the woods without the proper materials for such an event. I didn't look forward to sleeping on the ground or try sleeping in a tree. I believe that a little knowledge can go a very long way; listen and learn."

As he continued to regale his tale, I inhaled all of the information with great interest and learned that my husband has always been an entertaining man. He gets most of the things that he displays from conversing with other adults who have lived and who love to share knowledge.

Carl continued perfecting his method of preparing for the next big hunt. Carl has always stated that he is known for bringing home the bacon, as many would say.

My husband loves to hunt. I consider him to be a wild meat connoisseur. He is a hunter who is good at catching and consuming wild meats. We now have enough wild animals in our freezer to last our family for at least two years.

Carl still practices his ritual during the hunting season each year with his cousin Johnny. He and Johnny are forever meeting and plotting their next adventure in the forest to bag a deer, maybe a ten pointer. Oh, the many tales that I could relay, but time will not allow me to now, because it is the end of summer and fall hunting season is about to begin again.

Reflections 6

He's Hanging Out!

Knock, knock, knock! "Hello is someone home? It's Johnny, coming in!"

As I move toward Johnny's voice and his knocking, he is already in the house.

"Hi, Johnny," I said.

"Hey, Jane," he said.

"How are you doing, Johnny?"

"Jane, I'm fine; and you?"

"I am fine too," said Jane. "Carl, Johnny is here!" I called out.

Carl enters the room. Carl and Johnny mumble their pleasantries as they move toward the kitchen area to discuss their plans for the day.

"Everyone is just relaxing and enjoying the day," Johnny states.

"Yeah Johnny, we are just enjoying the day. Come on in. It's another beautiful day in the neighborhood. This hunting season is going to be great!" Carl says.

"Man, have you heard that there are some big deer up in north Georgia?" Johnny asked.

"No, man," Carl responded.

Carl and Johnny go on to explain their plan for hunting in the mountains of north Georgia.

Mind you, my husband Carl usually hunts on his family land in Alabama or scouts near West Point, Georgia. In these locations, he is less likely to run into a bear or even fall off a cliff while trying to bag a deer. If he decides to hunt in north Georgia, I'll now have to worry about cliffs or hillbillies. They could run the risk of running into a moonshiner's organization. Man, what trouble one could find so far from home. If he decides to hunt in north Georgia, I'll have to now worry about bears too.

Reflecting upon my husband's new location for hunting, I noticed my husband and his cousin slowly move into the backyard of our home. They sat and talked for some time about their hunting trip to north Georgia this coming fall. Usually, I wouldn't fret too much about his hunting on his family land in Alabama or even hunting in central Georgia, but north GA… north Georgia is very mountainous. There are lots of cliffs, sharp overhangs, rocky hills, deep gorges, rivers, deep terrain, mountain lions, and black bears. I can just imagine him getting attacked by a hungry, angry bear.

He tells me all the time, "People are stupid to go into the woods without a weapon."

He would say, "They are just serving themselves up as a happy meal."

I would laugh, then tell him not to be so negative.

He retorts with, "You'll never catch me in the wood without a gun. Bang! We'll be eating some good old bear meat." We'd laugh until our sides hurt.

On this particular day, they were planning their next trip, possibly to the north Georgia mountains. As I sit in the kitchen, I could hear them planning their trip.

I could barely make out what they were doing with their checklist of things that they should have for their next trip.

Deer pee	Check
Gun/bullets	Check
Boots	Check
Deer salt	Check
Antlers	Check
Sleeping bag	Check
Warmers	Check
Rations	Check
Long johns	Check
Gloves	Check
Crossbow and arrows	Check
Hunting license	Check and double check

These are just a few of the things that they mentioned in the conversation. They talked for some time as they made plans for their upcoming hunting trip.

Suddenly, I hear my husband say, "Hey Man, toss me that rope."

My interest was piqued because if they were sitting and talking, why would my husband need a rope. What were they doing? The talking had stopped. As I moved toward the window, I peered out. I could see that Carl, my husband, had climbed up on a deer stand that he had repaired and anchored to a pine tree in the back yard. He yells down to his cousin to throw him a line. Johnny tosses it up to him. As he does so, Carl leans out to grab it with no thought of his safety. Carl failed to harness himself safely to the ladder. He does this without any safety attachment. My eyes widen with shock. Has he lost his mind? He knows better than to climb a ladder without using his safety harness. God! He is going to fall and break his neck.

I immediately raised the kitchen window and yelled out.

"Get off of that ladder, now, before you fall and kill yourself."

He laughs, reaches out and grabs it again. Why they needed it, I had no idea, but it and Carl go flying without care. He does it once again, and I scream. He looks towards the window and laughs.

"Cuz," Johnny says, "For a minute there, Carl, I thought you were going to fall. Man, that was close and quick."

"Yeah man," he states. "I better get down before my wife has a heart attack."

After securing the rope, Carl looked back at the kitchen window in which I was standing. I yell out at him, "Carl get down, get out of that tree and off of that ladder, now. If you fall off that ladder or out of that tree and break your neck, I'll beat your behind. Now get down."

Carl and Johnny looked at each other, shook their heads, and roared out with laughter. They both just chuckled and continued to plan another adventure.

I stepped away from the window, shaking with anger. I realized Carl was not taking my warning seriously. Well, I thought to myself, if he falls, I'll just leave him out there to stew for a while. I quickly rethought that idea. I shook my head as I laughed softly to myself.

Resuming my many tasks in the home, I continued to hear the two men talking and laugh about their upcoming hunting trip.

He'll Shop Til' He Drops

"Oh, man! Babe, I just found my gift card for the Bass Pro Shop that our kids gave me for my last birthday. I forgot all about it."

"What gift card? Where was it?" I asked.

"I was searching through some of my hunting pants and ran across it," he stated.

I asked, "How did you get this?"

Looking closely at the card, I slowly gave

it to Carl. Carl took the card from me as he mumbled something about receiving from the kids.

Jokingly I said, "You got a gift card from the kids that you claim that you don't know."

He laughs and said, "You know that I love my kids."

I stated in a humorous tone, "I am just saying. You shouldn't disown our kids."

He and I laughingly bantered with each other for a little while longer. He walked to the living room closet and pulled his jacket and hat out of the closet and began putting them on.

I asked, "Where are you going?"

"I am going shopping," he said. "I am going to use my gift card now."

I chimed into his plans, "I want to go."

He says, "Let's go."

Thank God, our children were spending

the day with a relative. So off we went to the Bass Pro Shop in Gwinnett County. This was the nearest shop to our location.

As we exited the house, my cell phone rang. I was reluctant to answer it, but I had to remember that I am a mother, and someone else is looking after them. To my surprise, it was my husband sister, Tina; my kids were being treated to a sleepover at Tina's house. I was hoping that she would keep them an extra day, but knowing her, she probably had run out of food. My boys could eat. They eat all day long.

I responded to the call, and to my disappointment, Tina asked how long would it take for me to pick up my kids or that she would drop them off. I told her that she could drop them off at any time. She agreed to do just that as soon as possible. This gave me time to prepare a snack for them just before dinner so that they would not grow too hungry. Our phone conversation ended. I informed my husband that his sister was on her way to the house to drop off the kids.

He says, "Well, I guess you can't go. I'll see you later." Minutes later, he was off to the store.

I knew he wanted to go shopping. He needed to be able to shop in peace. I have always loved going to the Bass Pro Shop to purchase hunter's gear with my husband, Carl. I simply enjoy sitting and watching the massive aquarium tank that they have on display in the store. This humongous aquarium is a favorite crowd pleaser and a calming mechanism for parents with children. Once they lay sight on the big tank, they immediately stop in their tracks and just gawk at the attraction in amazement. This gives most parents a break from their disruptive kids. Watching the fish swim around the tank is very relaxing.

Suddenly, remembering the time, I had become aware of the fact that my husband has been gone for some time. Quickly, I glanced at my cell phone to see if he had called. My phone registered no calls. I looked out into the yard for his car, no car. I said out loud, "Where is this, man?"

Carl was thrilled to have received such a thoughtful gift from his children. I know he went shopping, but more than three hours had passed, and Carl has not returned. What was he buying in the store? I don't recall the kids putting that much money on the card. It had just about two hundred dollars. How much can you buy with that amount?

Oops! I forgot he is a thrifty shopper. He can go to the store to spend a hundred dollars or less and obtain all of the necessary things to complete a meal and not go over the budget by a penny. He purchases only what is on the list. If it is not in the budget, then it is not being purchased. It would have to be added to the wishlist - I wish I had bought that.

Finally, as the clock continues to tick away – tick tock, tick tock, I heard, "Babe, I am home!"

I looked out of the back kitchen window, and to my surprise, I saw a plastic deer standing and staring back at me. It was standing in the middle of the yard. I was drawn closer to the kitchen window to get a better look. Yes, a large plastic deer was standing upright in the yard. I heard my husband talking to it as if it was going to talk back. I left the window and moved into the back yard. I could hear and see the gleefulness coming from my husband. He happily put away the many things that he had purchased from the Bass Pro Shop.

As I approached him, I asked. "What is this, and what are you doing?"

"Babe, I have hit the jackpot! Meet my friend Lucy."

Lucy, as he called it, was a four-foot plastic deer. It was brown with a white underbelly. It had two pointed ears with black tips. It had eyes that never moved but just stared into space or at you, if you happened to stand in front of it. Yes, Lucy was the size of a Great Dane.

He said, laughing, "This baby is going to help me with my archery practice. I am going to place her over here in the bushes. That way, I will have the effect of hunting," he goes on to say.

I just stood and listened in amazement. He went on for forty-five minutes with his unpacking and placing his newly purchased gear in our storage shed. After some time, all that I saw was an unusual object peering out of the shrubbery in the back yard.

I turned and walked back toward the house.

He yelled after me, "I'll be in the house in a few minutes."

I just waved my hand and walked into the house. Minutes later, in walked my husband with his arms full of hunting gear. He plopped them onto the dining room table.

He went into a long, drawn out, detailed speech of what was purchased, why, how much it cost, and most of all, how it makes him look and feel when he uses it. I was so uninterested in this monologue, but as a dutiful wife, I listened patiently, as I usually did.

He continued to unpack and put away the things that he purchased. I started noticing the amount and quality of the items that he bought. I knew he had a gift card with a limit, but this was seeming to cost a lot. Let Carl tell it, he got a deal, and everything was on sale at a reduced price. One thing about my husband, he does know how to manage his pennies.

Pondering about the amount of money that he may have spent shopping, I suddenly realized that my husband was bragging about how much money he saved buying various hunting gear at a discounted price.

"I only spent less than seventy-five bucks for all of these things," Carl stated, smiling.

I smiled back. "That's great dear. You have always been frugal when it comes to spending money," I said.

"Once I snag a deer, we will save even more money because we will have lots of meat to put into the freezer for the winter. We'll have meat for soups, burgers, meat-loaf, spaghetti, you name it. Babe, this year, I think that I am going to get that ten-point buck. I can see it now. I am going to mount the antlers in front of the storage shed. Yeah, they will look nice there," he states. "I have everything that I can possibly need. I am prepared."

We looked at each other lovingly. I thought to myself, "Carl will get that prized buck this winter."

Carl gathered the remaining items that were on the kitchen table and marched off to the shed in the back yard. I rose from my chair and watched him from the kitchen window as he went in and out of the stor-age shed.

Reflections 8

It's Guarding the Homestead

Carl's hunting paraphernalia was stored away and was waiting patiently for the new hunting season to begin. Oh my, I forgot about the giant plastic deer that continued to stand and guard our back yard. In the dark, it gives an ominous and threatening presence to anyone who enters our property. My husband left it standing in front of our utility shed. It stood as if it was guarding it. It stood tall and straight as if it was ready to strike at any threat that entered our grounds. Most people think that it is a large dog when they come to the house.

Several of our close friends continually asked, "Do you all have a dog?"

"Hey man, put away your dog! or Wow, what a large dog!"

We would just chuckle and tell them that it wasn't a dog, but a fake deer. Once our friends realized that the deer was not real, they would be surprisingly shocked then they would have to go and see it up close for themselves. Some would even just touch it or rub on it while laughing at their short-comings of not be able to recognize a plastic deer from a dog. It became a conversation piece for some time.

I'll never forget one time when my eldest brother stopped by our home while we were away. He later called saying, "Y'all better tie-up that big dog in the back yard. If he gets out, he'll bite someone or even a child. Someone is going to go to jail."

I said, "Man, what are you talking about?"

His response, "I am talking about that large dog in your back yard."

"Honey, we do not have a dog. That is a large plastic hunting deer that Carl bought from the Bass Pro Shop. I don't know what you were looking at. Did you have your glasses on?" I asked, laughing.

He responded, "For real, it looked so real. Maybe, I do need to wear my glasses more." My brother laughed softly at himself.

Another incident took place when some close family friends came to visit one evening but refused to get out of their car because they thought we had a dog. They sat in their vehicle and honked their horn for help.

We asked, "Why are you blowing your horn, come on into the house."

They responded, "We were afraid that it would bite us. Some dogs are vicious, and biting isn't a problem for them. We don't want to get bit. That's why we called and asked if you had a dog?"

"What, dog? We do not have a dog. That is a plastic hunting deer that Carl purchased from a hunting store."

Once they were able to see for themselves that it wasn't real, they were very relieved. We all laughed and went into the house and resumed our visit. As we entered the house, I glanced at my husband face. He was smiling broadly as if they made this giant plastic deer just for him. To this day, I have yet to see him shoot an arrow at it. It only stands in the yard guarding its space or looking as if it is defending its territory.

Reflections 9
He's Exploring New Territory

Carl and Johnny were ready for a new year, a new season, a new adventure and once again the hunting season started with this duo hunting team, Carl and Johnny. Packing and searching for a host of hunting paraphernalia: knives, boots, rifles, bows with arrows, etc. the duo plan, plot and synchronize their effort in gathering thoughts and preparing for the next episode of a hunting expedition.

This hunting trip began in December. My husband and his cousin made plans to hunt on a friend's land in Central Georgia. Usually, they would scout land near West Point Lake in South Georgia. But this particular trip was different because they made plans to go in a new area or region. This new area was farther south, but just as thick and dense as the land that our family owned in Alabama.

Recalling his many tales of encountering all kinds of critters during hunting, I reflected upon an incident in which they were confronted with several poisonous snakes. On this particular day trip, they ran across several cottonmouth rattlesnakes. They knew that they would come across some snakes, but they weren't expecting them to be so close and numerous to their hunting area. During their tracking of prey, they came across several cottonmouth rattlesnake skins. Thank God they packed their snake chaps and snake repellant for extra safety while hunting on the new grounds.

As they traveled several yards, they saw evidence of snake beds, skin, or an old snake rattle that had broken off. Yes, they seemed to be in a snake den. Neither hunter enjoyed the extra danger, but they were determined to wrangle a buck this hunting season. They refused to return home without a catch. They did not come this far to return home with an empty coffer. So, tread on they did, deeper into the forest. They moved over several deer trails. They took extreme caution because of the many snake sightings. They were cautious around bushes, rocks, boulders or any object that could possibly hide snakes.

While searching high and low for possible snakes, they overlooked the path and distance that they had traveled. Before long, they were deep into the woods. If bitten, they would have to go a long way back to their camp as well as their vehicle. Keeping this in mind, they marched on with great eagerness to bag a deer. So, as they continued to move into the forest, they kept an eye out for their arch enemy - snakes. But a few more miles and time, their patience and endurance paid off. They snagged a deer.

Once the deer was down, they immediately checked the area for snakes. Once that was done, they began the preparation for gutting, skinning, and dissecting the valuable parts for eating. Such elements consist of the following: ribs, shoulders, hindquarters, liver, kidneys, antlers, and the legs too. All other parts are left for the scavengers to feed on in the woods. Now, they must begin packing and transporting the meat to the camp and then the car. Having the deer carcass dissected and packed took another hour because carrying a fresh-killed animal must be handled with care, and it is very time-sensitive.

Upon returning to camp, they broke it down within fifteen minutes after storing their gear and their fresh catch into the back of the vehicle. They loaded up the deer meat and off they went. Homeward bound with their prized possession - deer meat. They were on their way home to show and share what they were able to bag.

They were genuinely content with leaving the woods and without getting bitten by a snake. They were relieved and chatty on their drive home. Not once did they turn on the car radio or make a phone call back home. This upset me because I had not heard from him for almost a week. Carl calling and informing me that he was alright would have been a polite thing to do, but I know my husband, he gets sidetracked when he and his cousin are hunting.

One week and twelve hours later, my hunting team arrived home safely. I heard them exit the vehicle and walk toward the house. I opened the door but only caught a glimpse of them heading toward the back yard. Minutes later, I heard them regale about their adventure. Carl and Johnny laughed and talked for hours as they put away the deer meat. I listened silently to them as they recounted over and over their narrow escape from the poisonous snakes. I was so pleased that they made it home safely.

Reflections 10
He Concludes

Carl and Johnny's hunting season is over, and the hunting year ended on a reasonable and high note for the two hunters. Snagging a deer this past hunting season was an excellent achievement for Carl and his cousin. They will have meat for a long time to share with the family.

Carl and Johnny slowly and meticulously stored away their hunting gear. They talked and teased each other about their hunting styles. As they laughed, they placed hunting bins all over the backyard. They compiled their hunting gear into one and then another; within an hour, all bins were packed, stacked, and put in their appropriate storage spaces. His cousin, Johnny, stored some of his gear in our shed. We didn't and don't mind because he spends most of his time at our house anyway.

I heard them say they're good-byes to each other.

"See you later, cuz," Carl said

"Alright, see you later," Johnny responded.

As Carl and Johnny conclude another year of hunting adventure, I am reminded that my husband Carl and his cousin Johnny have been hunting partners since they were small children in Camphill, Alabama. These two men were forever scouting and tracking down their prey and bringing home all kinds of fresh meat to eat. They would kill the following: rabbit, pheasant, dove, raccoon, deer, turtle, quail, etc. These two men are forever joined. To this day, they are forever planning for their next adventure in the woods.

P.O. Box 453

Powder Springs, Georgia 30127

www.entegritypublishing.com

info@entegritypublishing.com

770.727.6517